A Case of Sense

by Songju Ma Daemicke

illustrated by Shennen Bersani

On a summer day, Ming was playfully racing a wheel down the city street with a stick.

When passing Fu Wang's big house, Ming was greeted by strong and delicious cooking smells and the sounds of clanging pots and frying pans. This was unusual. Ming was alarmed and stopped his wheel. What was the greedy Fu Wang up to today?

Suddenly, a loud cry flew out. "Neighbors, your attention please! We are cooking eight wonderful dishes for you today!" The gong sounded.

Bong!

"Steamed Fish!"

Bong!

"Fried Shrimp!"

Bong!

"Beef Stew!"

"Kungpao Chicken!"

Bong!

Bong!

Ming soon recognized the voice as that of Fu Wang.

Ming's father rushed over. He dragged him back home and closed the door behind them.

Later that afternoon, Fu Wang's voice was heard again. "Neighbors, an important announcement! I have prepared the wonderful aromas of many fine dishes today for your enjoyment. Tomorrow morning, I will collect forty cents per family as payment. Have your money ready!"

Ming now understood Fu Wang's greedy purpose.

The following morning, Ming watched Fu Wang as he went door to door, loudly demanding money. The residents refused to pay him.

"I will take all of you to court!" Fu Wang threatened. "Then you will have to pay me even more or go to jail."

The next day, people who lived within two blocks of Fu Wang, including Ming's parents, were ordered to appear in the local city court. Ming and many other curious folk came along.

Ming made his way to the front of the packed court room. The accused neighbors stood silently on the left. Fu Wang stood on the opposite side of the bench.

The judge whacked his gavel on the bench three times.

Bam!

Bam!

Bam!

"Silence!" he demanded. "Fu Wang, state the reason you claim you are owed money."

Fu Wang spoke with confidence. "I hired helpers to cook many foods, allowing my neighbors to enjoy the delicious aromas of eight different dishes for an entire day. Now they should pay me for my planning, the food, and the labor of my cooks."

The judge turned to the accused residents. "What is your response?"

One neighbor came forward. "I did not smell his food. I was inside all day."

Fu Wang barked, "Impossible! The aromas were everywhere. You could not avoid them!"

One young man said furiously, "The smells from Fu Wang's food were not something we asked for. Why should we pay for them?"

The judge said nothing as both sides argued back and forth. Finally, the judge banged down his gavel.

The judge faced the accused residents. "Check your pockets for coins! As I call each one of you, bring forty cents to my bench."

The neighbors looked defeated and shook their heads in disbelief. Ming felt sad for them. Fu Wang victoriously folded his arms.

The judge stood up. "Fu Wang, come to my bench!"

The judge then called out a name from the list of the accused. "Bin Chen, come to my bench and bring your coins."

A nervous old man stood in front of the judge.

"Now stand close to Fu Wang, and shake and rattle your coins as loudly as you can," said the judge.

Bin Chen did as he was told.

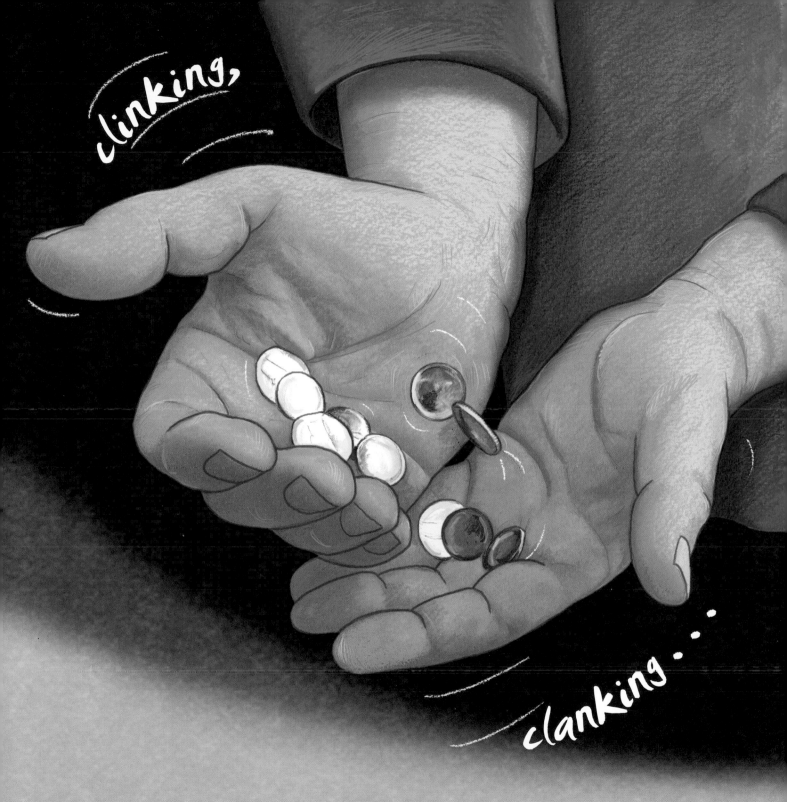

The sound of coins in his trembling
hands seemed somber and heavy.

The judge waved his hand. "Stop!"

Then he turned to Fu Wang. "Did you hear the sound of Bin Chen's coins?"

"Yes, I did." Fu Wang leaned forward,
ready to make the coins his own.

The judge said simply, "You have now collected your payment from Bin Chen."

Fu Wang seemed confused. "I don't understand."

The judge said firmly, "You have been paid for what Bin Chen smelled with the sound of his coins."

He turned to Bin Chen. "You can now step back."

Fu Wang's mouth dropped open. Ming laughed out loud at the sheer logic of this order.

The judge then called out the next person.
"Hua Zhang, bring your coins to my bench."

This time, the sound of the coins seemed
light and happy.

clinking,

clanking . . .

One by one, all the accused neighbors
joined in shaking their own coins.

clinking, clanking, clinking, clanking . . .

Finally, the court room quieted down and the judge stood up. "Neither smell nor sound has definite shape or volume. Once created, they are passed freely through the air. All people nearby will receive them passively. The sound of the coins is a fair trade for the smell of the food. The case is now closed!"

The city folk cheered. Ming, impressed by the fairness of this decision, decided he would work hard to become a wise judge himself one day.

For Creative Minds

Senses

People learn about the world around them through senses. There are five senses that most people share: sight, hearing, taste, smell, and touch. Some people have senses that work differently (many people wear glasses to help their sense of sight) or have fewer than five senses.

Match the senses to the body part.

ears

eyes

nose

skin

tongue

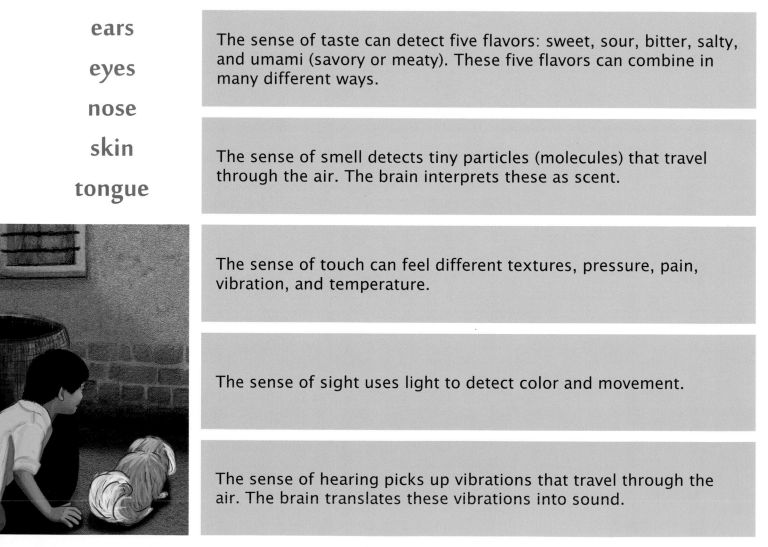

The sense of taste can detect five flavors: sweet, sour, bitter, salty, and umami (savory or meaty). These five flavors can combine in many different ways.

The sense of smell detects tiny particles (molecules) that travel through the air. The brain interprets these as scent.

The sense of touch can feel different textures, pressure, pain, vibration, and temperature.

The sense of sight uses light to detect color and movement.

The sense of hearing picks up vibrations that travel through the air. The brain translates these vibrations into sound.

Answer: ears-hearing, eyes-sight, nose-smell, skin-touch, tongue-taste

Match the Sound

Match the sound with its source.

bam

bark

bong

clink-clank

knock

meow

1.

2.

3.

4.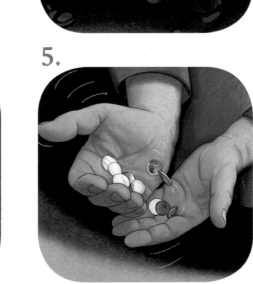

5.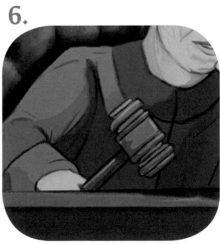

6.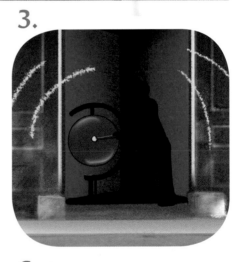

Answers: 1-dog, bark. 2-cat, meow. 3-gong, bong. 4-door, knock. 5-coins, clink-clank. 6-gavel, bam.

Smell

What objects on this page have a strong smell?
What objects have little or no smell?

What objects on this
page do you think
would smell good?
Are there any that you
think would smell bad?

How can you describe smells?
What words would you use to tell
someone what something smells like
or to compare two different smells?

What can you smell from
a distance? What things
do you have to be close
to in order to smell?

Diffusion

When Fu Wang asked his cooks to prepare many delicious meals, the smell spread out the windows and down the street. Soon all the neighbors in the city could smell the food. This is called **diffusion**.

Diffusion is when something spreads out from an area of high concentration to an area of low concentration. Smell is carried by molecules in the air. The smell of Fu Wang's food was highly concentrated in the kitchen, where the cooks were working. The molecules spread out of the kitchen and down the street, to areas of lower concentration. Eventually a smell diffuses so much that it is barely noticeable.

Diffusion in action

You can observe diffusion by adding food coloring to liquid and watching how it spreads.

For this process you will need:
- bowl
- food coloring
- water

Pour water into your bowl. Add a few drops of food coloring. Watch what happens and write down your observations.

After you are finished observing, pour the water down the drain.

Think about it: Would the colors diffuse the same way in different liquids, like syrup, milk, or a smoothie? What if you added soap or oil along with the food coloring? Come up with more questions about diffusion. Create your own experiments to test your hypotheses.

To both my grandpa and my late parents. My grandpa planted the seed of this story in my mind and my father instilled the love of the storytelling in me when I was a little girl!—SMD

To my cousin, Dorothy Hartnett, whose weekly phone call keeps me connected to my roots. Love ya, Cuz.—SB

Thanks to Rachel Carpenter, Education Manager of The Children's Discovery Museum of Normal, IL, for verifying the accuracy of the information in this book.

Library of Congress Cataloging-in-Publication Data

Names: Daemicke, Songju Ma, author. | Bersani, Shennen, illustrator.
Title: A case of sense / by Songju Ma Daemicke ; illustrated by Shennen Bersani.
Description: Mount Pleasant, SC : Arbordale Publishing, 2016. | Summary: When greedy Fu Wang takes his neighbors to court for enjoying the aroma of food he had prepared, a wise judge inspires young Ming to become a judge himself, one day. Includes activities.
Identifiers: LCCN 2016018815 (print) | LCCN 2016019516 (ebook) | ISBN 9781628558524 (english hardcover) | ISBN 9781628558531 (english pbk.) | ISBN 9781628558555 (english downloadable ebook) | ISBN 9781628558579 (english interactive dual-language ebook) | ISBN 9781628558548 (spanish pbk.) | ISBN 9781628558562 (spanish downloadable ebook) | ISBN 9781628558586 (spanish interactive dual-language ebook) | ISBN 9781628558555 (English Download) | ISBN 9781628558579 (Eng. Interactive) | ISBN 9781628558562 (Spanish Download) | ISBN 9781628558586 (Span. Interactive)
Subjects: | CYAC: Greed--Fiction. | Wisdom--Fiction.
Classification: LCC PZ7.1.D23 Cas 2016 (print) | LCC PZ7.1.D23 (ebook) | DDC [E]--dc23
LC record available at https://lccn.loc.gov/2016018815

Translated into Spanish: *Un case con sentido común*
Lexile® Level: AD 550L
Keywords: civics, community, logic, senses (hearing, smell), diffusion

Manufactured in China, May 2016
This product conforms to CPSIA 2008
First Printing

Arbordale Publishing
Mt. Pleasant, SC 29464
www.ArbordalePublishing.com